SEPHIR
THE
STORM MONSTER

With special thanks to Michael Ford
For Henry Nettleton, brave and true

www.beastquest.co.uk

ORCHARD BOOKS
338 Euston Road, London NW1 3BH
Orchard Books Australia
Level 17/207 Kent St, Sydney, NSW 2000

A Paperback Original
First published in Great Britain in 2009
This edition published in Great Britain in 2014

Beast Quest is a registered trademark of Beast Quest Limited
Series created by Beast Quest Limited, London

Text © Beast Quest Limited 2009
Cover and inside illustrations by Steve Sims
© Orchard Books 2009

A CIP catalogue record for this book is available
from the British Library.

ISBN 978 1 40833 589 5
1 3 5 7 9 10 8 6 4 2
Printed in Slovakia by TBB

Cover repro by Saxon Photolitho, Norwich, Norfolk
The paper and board used in this paperback are natural recyclable
products made from wood grown in sustainable forests.
The manufacturing processes conform to the environmental
regulations of the country of origin.

Orchard Books is a division of Hachette Children's Books,
an Hachette UK company.

www.hachette.co.uk

The National Literacy Trust is a registered charity no: 1116260 and
a company limited by guarantee no. 5836486 registered in England
and Wales and a registered charity in Scotland no. SC042944.
Registered address: 68 South Lambeth Road, London SW8 1RL.
National Literacy Trust logo and reading tips © National Literacy
Trust 2014
www.literacytrust.org.uk/donate

SEPHIR
THE
STORM MONSTER

BY ADAM BLADE
INSPIRED BY KIERON CAMERON

ORCHARD

THE ICY

TH

THE NORTHERN MOUNTAINS

THE FOREST OF FEAR

WESTERN OCEAN

T

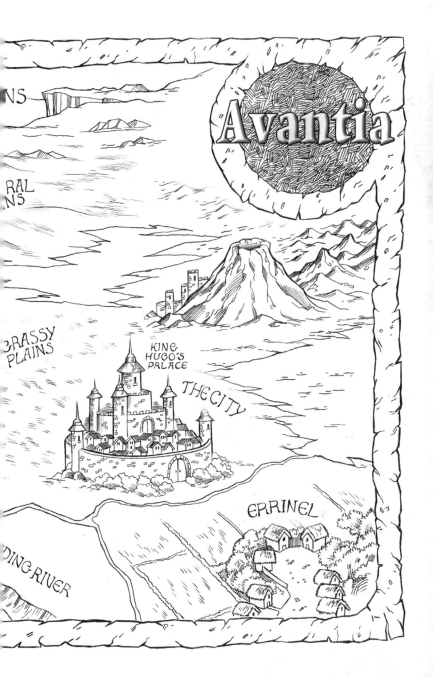

Greetings, and welcome to the Kingdom of Avantia. I am Aduro, wizard of King Hugo's realm. I come to tell you that a time of great peril is upon us.

Once every generation, a battle must take place, the likes of which your world will never see. The chosen Master of the Beasts has to take on the Dark Wizard, Malvel, for the ultimate prize: the Book of Worlds.

Should the Book fall into evil hands, there is no telling the death and destruction that may entail.

The Master of the Beasts has nothing on his side but courage and the support of his loyal companions. Will that be enough to defeat Malvel's greatest evil yet?

There is only one way of finding out...

Aduro

PROLOGUE

"What is it, boy?" said Simon, Avantia's shepherd. His dog Max's ears were pressed back, and he was looking west towards the mountains.

Over the hills, Simon could see what he thought was a bird. But it was huge!

The shape sailed through the sky, getting closer, as the sheep nervously huddled together.

It became bigger and stretched into a column. As a howling sound screeched in Simon's ears, he finally realised what he was looking at.

A tornado – heading straight for the flock!

Simon looked around desperately for somewhere to hide. A huge oak tree grew at the edge of the meadow. He ran towards it.

"Max!" he shouted. He gave a series of short whistles, and Max darted behind the flock, guiding the sheep towards the sheltering branches.

The noise of the twister had become a roar, and the air was suddenly cold.

Simon could see debris caught in the walls of the tornado, whipped up and spinning in the wind.

Wait. There was something else.

As the column bulged, shapes began to form in the coils of the twister.

Simon could see the hollows of two eyes…the curl of a sneer… It was a face!

The tornado was closing in on him fast. Its mouth gaped open, and a terrible scream filled Simon's ears.

The wind slammed into the oak tree.

Simon felt his body being lifted from the ground. He clutched at the empty air until his fingers closed on something – a branch! He hung on, the wind whipping his body upwards and wrenching his arms. Beneath him, he could see his sheep being flung across the mountain.

With a final wail, the storm passed. Simon dared to look around him.

The tree had been stripped bare.

There was no sign of the flock, other than the odd scrap of white fleece among the debris.

Shaking, Simon clambered to the ground.

"Max!" he called out.

There was no answer.

"Max! Where are you, boy?"

Still nothing. Simon staggered down the hillside. His best friend and his precious herd had gone forever.

He fell to his knees. Whatever was driving that tornado was evil to the core…

CHAPTER ONE

A CHALLENGE LIKE NO OTHER

Tom and Elenna were riding across the plains of Avantia. Tom kicked his heels into Storm's jet-black flanks and his stallion charged forwards, his mane rippling in the air. Silver the wolf ran fluidly beside them.

Tom tugged on Storm's reins and the horse slowed to a canter as he climbed a small slope to a cluster of boulders.

Silver threaded between the rocks, his pink tongue lolling.

"Look," said Elenna, pointing. "That rock doesn't seem right."

Tom followed the line of her finger, and saw that one of the rocks was vibrating, as though there was an earthquake. But the ground beneath his feet wasn't moving. Silver gave a series of nervous barks.

The boulder suddenly seemed to melt, then changed shape, becoming a tall column.

"Stay back," said Tom to Elenna, pulling his sword from its scabbard.

The shifting rock took on the shape of a body.

"What are you?" he demanded.

A chuckle answered him. "You won't need a sword."

Tom recognised the voice. "Aduro!"

It was the good wizard who'd
helped them on their Beast Quests.
The rock changed again, becoming
the bright cloth of Aduro's robe.
Suddenly he was before them, in
the flesh.

"I'm sorry to have startled you.
I come with an important challenge,"
said the wizard, his face serious.

"Another Beast Quest?" Tom asked.

"Of a kind," said Aduro. "Let me show you something."

The wizard waved his hand, and the air beside him shimmered. An image appeared. In a snowy wasteland, a great white-haired Beast, with yellow claws and a furry face, was gripping a man in its fist.

"That's Nanook!" cried Elenna, recognising the snow monster they had rescued on an earlier Quest.

The man in the image was brandishing a sword. Suddenly, a dragon swooped into the picture and released a spurt of fire. The man lifted his shield and the flames bounced off the surface. Nanook roared and lifted the man higher still. He sliced with his sword, hacking at the dragon's scales. Then, with another wave of Aduro's hand, the image faded away.

16

"That was the Battle of the Beasts," the wizard explained, "held once every generation between the forces of good and evil. The Master of the Beasts must fight his arch enemy – and each may choose a Beast to help him. Now, Tom, it is your turn."

"But who is my arch enemy?" asked Tom.

"It has to be Seth," said Elenna. With a dreadful feeling of certainty, Tom knew his friend was right. He nodded. The boy Seth was Malvel's champion and loyal servant. He and Tom had had swordfights almost to the death.

"What's that?" asked Tom, pointing. A shimmering image of a leather-bound book had appeared by Aduro's side. It had gilt edges and a silver lock on the front.

"This," said Aduro, "is the Book of

Worlds, sent to Avantia by Kieron the Great many moons ago. It is what you will be duelling for. Its pages contain many secrets about the kingdom of Avantia and the worlds beyond. It can be used for great good, or great evil. It must never fall into Malvel's hands."

Tom couldn't remember ever seeing an object so beautiful. What secrets were hiding among its pages?

"I won't let you down," he said, his heart brimming with determination.

"It's time for you to select the Beast who will help you in the battle. Choose wisely," said Aduro.

Tom looked at the surface of his shield, where the tokens he had recovered from each of the good Beasts of Avantia were lodged: a fragment of horseshoe from Tagus the horse-man, a tooth from Sepron the sea serpent, a talon from Epos the flame bird, an eagle's feather from Arcta the mountain giant and a bell from Nanook. Each gave him a special power. His eye finally fell on the last token – Ferno's dragon scale.

All the tokens began glowing. As the shield lit up with rainbow colours, Tom saw six silhouettes appear on the horizon. Six Beasts – the first Beasts Tom had ever encountered. They had come to help him. He could see Arcta's shaggy fur and the snow-white pelt of Nanook the snow monster. Epos swooped through the air and Tagus pawed the ground. Tom laughed with joy to see them all again.

"Who will you choose?" asked Elenna, waving at their friends.

"I choose Ferno, fire dragon of the mountain!" Ferno was the first Beast Tom had ever come across, and it would be good to be reunited with him again.

He held out his shield and it vibrated on his arm.

Ferno flew up high into the sky, blotting out the sun, and the air was filled with an almighty roar of approval from the Beasts.

The dragon swooped towards them. His great dark wings beat the air, powering through the sky. With a toss of his spiky head, two jets of flame exploded from his nostrils.

Ferno was coming!

CHAPTER TWO

A SUPER-BEAST

"He's magnificent!" gasped Elenna.

"A good choice," said Aduro, smiling. The five remaining Beasts waved and turned away. They would help another day.

Ferno swooped low over the plain. Then he extended his black talons, landing gently on the rocks beside them. The smells of sulphur and soot were heavy in the air.

"Are you ready to face Malvel's evil again?" Tom asked the Beast.

The fire dragon lifted his head and sent out a jet of flames.

"Your bravery will be sorely tested, Tom," said Aduro. "Whatever it takes, Malvel must not get his hands on the Book. The whole of Avantia is relying on you."

Tom climbed along the hard ridges of Ferno's tail, then jumped onto the dragon's back between his wings.

"With Ferno and Elenna at my side," Tom said, "there's no way Seth will capture the Book of Worlds."

The dragon rose to his feet, with Tom holding on tight to his scales.

He looked down at Elenna and Aduro. Storm flicked his tail and whinnied, while Silver leapt up and down on the spot.

"Good luck, Tom!" Elenna cried, waving her hand in farewell. "I'm here if you need me."

Aduro lifted his hands, and there was a mighty *swoosh*. All around the horizon the sky changed colour, turning a darker shade of blue. It looked like a rainstorm, but the downpour was going upwards, climbing from the ground into the sky.

"What's that?" Tom asked.

"No one from Avantia must see the battle," said Aduro. "This magical rainstorm will shield it from their eyes. Seth will be here soon, and I must be gone. Goodbye, Tom, and good luck!"

Aduro's form folded in on itself. But instead of becoming a rock once more, what remained was a plinth. Resting on top was the Book of Worlds. Tom wondered if he should take the Book now, to keep it safe…

"Are you ready to die, Tom?" shouted a voice.

Seth! Ferno twisted round to face their enemy.

The wicked boy was riding a Beast of his own – a lion with three terrifying heads. It was Trillion, come back to life! The Beast bounded across the plain with Seth on his back. The boy's pale hair reflected the sunlight like marble and his cold blue eyes flashed. When he tugged on the lion's mane, all three sets of jaws opened with a deafening roar, revealing blood-stained teeth that were sharp enough to tear flesh.

Ferno took to the air. He flew low towards Seth and Trillion, his wing tips stroking the grass. Seth didn't move.

Tom smiled to himself. *This will be easier than I thought!*

A hiss split the air like a red-hot sword being plunged into water.

"Tom, look out!" Elenna screamed.

Something hammered into Tom's
stomach, throwing him clear of
Ferno's back. He slammed into the
ground, gasping for breath.

What was that?

A great shadow appeared and
Tom rolled out of the way just as a
slithering red and green tail thumped
the ground. Tom sprang to his feet,

and found himself face to face with
Vipero the snake man. Where had
he come from? Tom had already
defeated him once! Vipero's two snake
heads hissed through their poisonous
fangs. Tom drew his sword as one of
the heads darted towards him. The
blade glanced off the thick scales, and
Vipero slithered back towards Seth and
Trillion.

So that's Malvel's game, Tom thought.
Two Beasts against one.

Ferno landed beside him and Tom
leapt onto the dragon's back. A howl
echoed across the plain. Now a third
Beast was beside Seth and Trillion.
Thick brown fur covered its ape-like
face, and red bloodshot eyes glared out
at him.

Claw.

The giant monkey beat his massive

chest with two clawed arms, and the noise was like a drum. He howled again, showing his thick yellow teeth, and leapt into the air. Whatever evil magic Malvel was using, it looked like he was able to bring the evil Beasts of Gorgonia back to life – even after Tom had defeated them.

The three Beasts closed together. Claw climbed onto Vipero's back. Trillion moved in front of Vipero.

Tom blinked. *This can't be happening,* he thought.

The three Beasts were merging. Now there was only a single Beast where three had stood before. All that was left of the giant monkey were his long, bristling arms, ending in his razor-sharp claws. They were attached to the glistening, scaly body of Vipero. But instead of the snake man's snouts, it was the three heads of Trillion that stared back at Tom.

They let out a roar that vibrated through Tom's chest. Ferno circled the air and Tom saw Elenna place an arrow to her bow and train its point on the Beast's heart. But even from this distance, Tom could see her hand trembling.

Malvel had created a Super-Beast!

CHAPTER THREE

BENDING THE RULES

Ferno roared. With a few beats of his powerful wings, he and Tom were above Seth and the Super-Beast, hovering beneath Aduro's magic shield.

"Come down and fight!" shouted Tom's enemy. One of Claw's long monkey arms arced across the sky, missing Ferno by a whisker.

"Tom!" Elenna screamed.

He looked down and saw the earth beneath his companion's feet crumbling. Elenna struggled for balance, and then fell as the ground broke open. A girl with pale skin and jet-black hair burst out from the earth, carrying a shovel.

Sethrina, Seth's sister!

The rules of this game were changing all the time.

Before Elenna could right herself, Sethrina ran across the plain and climbed up Vipero's scaly coils to sit beside her evil brother. Tom guided Ferno back to the ground and landed beside Elenna. He slid from Ferno's back to help her up. The Super-Beast began thundering towards them.

"That's cheating!" Elenna said.

She grimaced as she climbed stiffly to her feet.

Sethrina sneered. "Ha! Your foolish magician may have placed a shield over the battle field, but he can't stop me digging underneath it."

"If they're going to ignore the rules, let's give them the same treatment," said Elenna. Ferno seemed to understand and extended a wing towards her. She ran up its length and Tom followed.

Now I'll do whatever it takes to win, Tom thought. He guided Ferno above their enemies.

"Too late!" called Seth, as the Super-Beast made for the plinth.

"After them, Ferno!" shouted Tom.

The Super-Beast had a head start, but its huge body lumbered along the ground, and Seth was fighting to control Trillion's three twisting heads.

"It looks like the Super-Beast may not be so great, after all," said Tom, grinning. Ferno darted after their enemies.

"Hurry, Ferno!" urged Tom. The Super-Beast extended a giant hairy arm towards the plinth. If Tom didn't get there soon…

An arrow whizzed past Tom's ear and embedded itself in Claw's limb. Trillion's three heads lifted as one, and growled in pain. Tom twisted round and saw that Elenna had her bow in her hand.

"Great shot, Elenna!" he said.

Sethrina jumped down from the Super-Beast and sprinted towards the plinth.

Elenna smiled grimly. "You take on Seth – I'll handle his sister. If we split up it will give us an advantage."

Tom directed Ferno down towards the plain. Elenna slipped off the Beast and landed in the grass beside Storm. In one fluid movement, she was up and onto the stallion's back. She fired two more arrows at Sethrina, who ducked behind a boulder.

Seth turned his Super-Beast to face Tom. Ferno dived, blasting jets of fire from his nostrils. The smell of singed hair filled the sky as Trillion's three heads roared in anger.

Ferno landed and ran through the grass towards their enemy. As he did so, Vipero's tail whipped around, and Tom lunged to one side as it sliced the air.

Trillion sank his teeth into Ferno's wing. The dragon bellowed and staggered backwards, clouds of black smoke drifting from his nostrils. Tom couldn't hold on, and was thrown off, landing hard.

"Ferno!" he shouted.

"Seems your Beast is no match for mine," mocked Seth. One of Claw's arms was around Tom's waist before he could stand, and he was lifted high in the air.

"Kill him!" shouted Seth.

Tom could hardly breathe, and his sword arm was trapped against his side. He was being lifted towards

Trillion's gaping jaws.

"Help!" he shouted, twisting desperately to find Elenna. She was struggling with Sethrina on the ground near the plinth.

Strings of saliva stretched between the Super-Beast's jagged teeth. Tom was so close he could smell the rotten stench of Trillion's breath. He jammed his shield inside the mouth of the nearest lion head. The jaws snapped shut, and splinters flew from Tom's shield. But it held firm!

"Devour him!" yelled Seth, furiously.

Suddenly a grey streak flashed by.

Silver!

Elenna's wolf leapt into the air and sank his teeth into Claw's arm.

The three heads roared simultaneously and Tom's shield clattered to the ground.

The grip around his waist loosened and he swiped with his sword at one of Trillion's massive necks. The blade hit home, blood spurting. Tom heaved his sword free and hacked again. Shrieking, the Super-Beast released its hold and Tom plummeted to the ground.

He looked up and saw the stricken Beast swaying back and forth. Vipero's tail lashed the grass in agony. With a flick of Claw's arm, Silver was sent flying, landing in the plains twenty paces away. But the wolf sprang straight up again.

The Super-Beast collapsed to one side and the ground shook. Seth cried out from beneath the mighty weight of the three merged bodies.

"Seth!" shouted Sethrina. "Brother?"

She rushed to where the Super-Beast

lay writhing in pain. Seth wriggled out from under it. As Tom watched, mesmerised, the three bodies of the evil Beast separated once more. Claw leapt up and down, cradling his injured arm, then ran away across the plain.

"Wait!" said Seth. "Where are you going? No!"

Vipero's twin heads gaped and hissed, his tongues forking in and out. The snake man detached himself, slithering off across the plain. He dived into the hole Sethrina had dug. Tom watched as the scaly tail disappeared.

"Stop!" said Seth. "Cowards!"

Trillion bounded away and smashed through the magic rainstorm.

The Beasts had fled; the battle was over.

"Seems like your Super-Beast has had enough," said Tom, coming to stand beside Elenna.

Sethrina looked at her brother in panic, but a slow smile crept across his lips. Doubt prickled at the back of Tom's mind.

"Now!" shouted Seth.

A shadow crept over them. Tom spun around. A great thundercloud was approaching at tremendous speed.

Silver howled, and backed away.

"What's happening?" whispered Elenna.

"I don't know," Tom hissed in reply.

It was a storm. Lightning flashed, scattering smoke and sparks through the air. Looming over them was the thick trunk of an enormous tornado, which was taller than King Hugo's castle. It swirled so fast it was a blur.

Then, gradually, a face formed
in the spinning winds – two eyes
and the curl of a sneer, from which
came the familiar sound of mocking
laughter…

"Malvel!" cried Tom.

The evil wizard's voice crackled
like thunder from amidst the bruised
clouds. "Behold your doom, Tom.
I am Sephir, monster of the storm!"

CHAPTER FOUR

THE HEART
OF THE STORM

Tom ran to where Ferno was waiting. He flung himself on the good Beast's back.

"Climb up next to me!" he called to Elenna. "We're dead if we try to fight Sephir on the ground."

Seth laughed. "You think you and your dragon are a match for Malvel's sorcery? There's no way you can tackle this Beast."

Elenna sprinted over and scrambled up beside Tom. Ferno thrashed his wings and they were airborne.

The air was suddenly cool as the sun disappeared behind the tornado. Sephir roared, and the sound was like a tempest at sea.

An arm made of whirling wind reached out from the body of the tornado as it drew closer. For a moment Tom thought they'd be crushed. But Ferno dodged to one side. The wind rushed past Tom, whipping up his hair as though fingers were snatching at him, threatening to drag him off the dragon's back.

He gripped Ferno's scales until his knuckles were white. They rose high above Sephir's head.

"Tom, the Book!" shouted Elenna.
Oh no!

Sephir's arm closed in on the plinth, causing the Book's pages to flutter wildly. Then the Book of Worlds was snatched up. It vanished into Sephir's dark heart, and he gave a roar of triumph that sounded like a screaming gale.

"It's over," Sethrina yelled gleefully over the noise. "The Book of Worlds is Malvel's!"

Tom stared into the spinning eddies of Sephir's body. Ferno circled the tornado, batting his wings hard to avoid being drawn in by the pull of the wind.

"If only I could get inside," Tom said.

"Inside?" asked Elenna.

"Sephir's not solid like a normal Beast," said Tom. "He's just air."

Tom steered Ferno over the top of Sephir, then carefully stood up on the dragon's back as he hovered above the tornado.

"What's your plan?" said Elenna, grabbing his arm.

"We're going into the heart of the storm. While there's blood in my veins, I won't let Malvel steal the Book of Worlds!"

Tom made sure his shield was tight across his back. It was now or never.

"Ready?" he said.

Elenna gripped his hand firmly. "Let's do this."

With his friend at his side, Tom leapt off Ferno's back and into the roaring winds below.

Sephir let out a cry of pain and anger, whipping around faster than ever before.

"No!" Tom heard Seth cry out in protest.

Tom plummeted like a rock, then turned upside down as the tornado seized him. He felt his limbs being flung about as he was spun round in the cyclone. When he managed to open his eyes, all he could see was a blur. Then he made out a shape opposite him.

Elenna!

She was pinned to the sides of the tornado, held by the sheer force of Sephir's fury. Tom felt sick with dizziness. A noise like a thousand wailing cats echoed in his ears. Sephir was in agony.

The winds writhed and turned, and it was impossible for Tom to get his bearings as they sank deeper inside. *Where's the Book?* he thought desperately.

Then suddenly the world was still.

Elenna floated beside him, cushioned on the air. He spotted the Book of Worlds being sucked through the empty space. Its gold-edged pages quivered violently and the spine was warped and broken, but the lock still held.

Tom dived after the Book, pulling himself with long strokes through Sephir's insides. The air was as chilly as a winter morning. He stretched out his fingers, and they brushed over the rough leather cover of the Book.

Almost there!

But the Book was whipped away in a sudden gust, and Sephir's laughter boomed.

"You don't have the strength," said Malvel's voice.

The cover of the Book of Worlds sprang open. Some of its pages were

ripped out, and flew off like leaves
tugged from a tree in a gale.

"You've failed," said Malvel's voice.
"The Book that your father almost
died for is mine. All Avantia will bow
before me!"

There must be something I can do,
thought Tom. *This Beast must have
a weakness!*

He drew his trusty blade, and with both hands on the hilt cut wide arcs through the air.

Malvel's cackle sounded again. "You can't hurt Sephir!"

Tom looked at Elenna, who was trying to grasp the torn pages of the Book of Worlds as they swirled around. He sheathed his sword.

Was it truly over? Had he let Aduro down? The air went cold again as the remaining pages spiralled away on the currents of air.

"Look, Tom!" Elenna shouted over the howling noise, pointing downwards with a stabbing gesture. "What's that?"

A blue light glowed below, right in the centre of the spiralling winds.

"I don't know," he called. "But I'm going to find out."

"The storm is more powerful down there," said Elenna. "You'll be ripped apart!"

"My golden armour will protect me," he said. The magical chainmail he had won on his Quest against Claw gave him strength of heart.

Tom turned and kicked through the raging winds. His clothes and hair streamed around him as he powered downwards. Each stroke was more difficult than the one before. The blue light became stronger, but so did the fury of the tornado.

It was like pushing through a blizzard. Tom felt ice crystals forming on his eyelashes. Thank goodness for Nanook's bell, embedded in his shield. With it, he was protected from the worst of the cold.

Tom's breath became rasping and

heavy. His heart thumped in his chest.

I won't give up, he thought. He kept his eyes fixed on the blue light. *Only a few more strokes…*

"Keep going, Tom!" called Elenna.

All around the tornado blasted him – it felt like being yanked in different directions by a hundred snatching hands. His arms burned.

Then the outer part of the blue orb shifted. In its shimmering surface, the features of a face appeared. A face Tom would recognise until the day he died.

Malvel.

So that was how the Dark Wizard controlled Sephir. Malvel dwelled at the heart of the storm, powering the Beast with his evil.

Suddenly new blasts of wind slammed into him, and Tom felt his teeth rattle in his head. He was being pushed backwards. The blue light became blinding.

"You're not strong enough," Malvel's cruel voice sneered. "Sephir will spit you out like a cherry stone."

Tom pulled his shield in front of him.

"Not this time," he said. If only he could reach the orb. He unsheathed his sword again.

It was now or never.

CHAPTER FIVE

THE BOOK
OF WORLDS

The wind smashed into his body like a giant invisible fist. The tornado tried to pluck his sword away, but Tom gripped the hilt until his hand throbbed. He lifted his arm above his head. Then he plunged his sword into the orb.

Tom's arm shook as energy surged up the blade. His whole body turned hot, and the air was filled with the smell of burning.

In the centre of the orb, Malvel's sneer disappeared. The howl of the winds was replaced by a shrill scream of horror. The blue light dimmed and vanished.

The spinning gales that had gripped Tom's body released their hold, and suddenly he could see sunlight again. The storm was passing.

A scream cut through the air above, and Elenna thudded into Tom. They both plummeted to the ground, and Tom saw the plains rush up to meet them. He managed to turn and get his shield beneath him. Arcta's magical feather slowed his descent and they landed softly in the grass.

"Are you all right?" asked Tom.

"I think so," Elenna said.

A shadow fell over them and Tom looked up. It was Storm! Tom used his stallion's reins to help him stand, and dusted himself down. Silver was licking Elenna's face. Her clothes were torn and her hair stuck up in all directions.

"Look at Sephir!" she said.

"Come back!" shouted Seth, waving his arms angrily. The storm monster was disintegrating before their eyes. "Where are you going?"

"Sephir's given up," said Tom. "Malvel's magic was all that was pushing him on."

"You're burnt," said Elenna.

Tom felt his hair. It was crispy and stiff.

"Malvel's evil must have passed through my sword," he said. "But I feel fine."

A thud made them both spin around. There, on the plinth, sat the tattered Book of Worlds.

"Oh, Tom," said Elenna. "Look at it. It's ruined."

She was right. Hardly any pages remained. The Book was ragged and torn and the cover was hanging off.

What have I done? thought Tom. He

walked slowly to the plinth. Even the silver lock on the front was dull and scratched.

"Tom, look!" said Elenna. She was pointing upwards. Tom saw what he thought was a bird in the sky, fluttering its wings.

It was joined by another.

"Wait a moment," said Tom. "They're not birds. They're…"

"…pages!" finished Elenna.

The pieces of parchment drifted out of the clouds. The first spiralled on a breeze, then settled perfectly back into the Book of Worlds. The others joined it, each lying in its rightful place.

"It can't be!" Sethrina shouted.

"What's happening?"

Elenna and Tom rushed over to the plinth.

Up close, the Book seemed to glow.
Now it looked like it had never been
moved.

Tom stroked the smooth leather
cover and gently opened the Book.
The first page was a map of Avantia,
drawn in bright colours and inscribed
with decorative script.

He turned it over.

"Gorgonia!" said Elenna.

Tom flicked through several more
pages. Each held a map more exotic

than the last. There was a map of Rion – a kingdom he had visited on a previous Quest. There were also lands he'd never heard of, let alone seen – places with names like Gwildor, Baltland and Marromore.

Could it be that each realm held Beasts of its own?

"No wonder Malvel wants the Book so badly," said Tom. "He could wreak havoc with all this information."

"Hey," shouted a voice. "Get this Beast away from us."

Seth and his sister gripped each other in terror as the fire dragon stood over them, his nostrils smoking.

"What shall we do with them?" asked Elenna. She gave Tom a wink.

"Maybe we should let Ferno toast them," said Tom, playing along.

"No, please," said Seth. "We didn't

mean any harm."

"We were just doing what Malvel told us," Sethrina added.

As much as he hated Seth and all he stood for, Tom couldn't let the pair be killed. That would make him no better than Malvel.

"Do you promise to leave Avantia and never come back?" he said.

Both nodded, looking nervously up at Ferno.

"Good," said Tom. "I'll arrange your transport." He looked at the fire dragon, who seemed to understand.

Ferno scooped the brother and sister up with his wing and dropped them onto his back. He blasted flames into the sky. Then, in three massive strides, he was airborne and beating his powerful wings. Storm and Silver came to stand beside Tom and Elenna,

and together they watched the Beast
disappear over the horizon.

I couldn't ask for more loyal friends,
Tom thought.

"Let's hope Ferno doesn't drop
them in the sea," said a voice.

Tom spun around and saw Aduro
stroking his long beard. In his other

hand was the Book of Worlds.

Elenna ran to throw her arms around the good wizard.

"The battle is over," said Aduro, smiling as Elenna hugged him. "You have made Taladon proud today, Tom."

"And Avantia is safe?" asked Elenna.

"Thanks to both of you," said Aduro.

All five of them turned to gaze over the rolling hills of Avantia. Aduro tucked the Book of the Worlds under his arm and began to fade away.

"I'll return this to safekeeping, where it belongs," he told Tom and Elenna, his voice becoming faint as he disappeared. They waved goodbye. Then Tom turned to face his friend.

"Are you ready for whatever happens next? There's sure to be another Quest soon," Tom said.

The sun was beginning to set over the horizon.

Elenna grinned. "I'll always be ready," she said. Silver leapt into the air, barking, and Storm bucked his back legs. Tom laughed as he led the way over to a flat patch of ground that would make a good camp for the night.

"Then let's see what the morning brings," he said. He was certain he and his friends would be called on again.

He couldn't wait!

=≫ **Series 1** ⋘=

COLLECT THEM ALL!

Have you read all the books in Series 1 of
BEAST QUEST? Read on to find out where
it all began in this sneak peek from book 1,
FERNO THE FIRE DRAGON...

978 1 84616 483 5

978 1 84616 482 8

978 1 84616 484 2

978 1 84616 486 6

978 1 84616 485 9

978 1 84616 487 3

CHAPTER ONE

THE MYSTERIOUS FIRE

Tom stared hard at his enemy. "Surrender, villain!" he cried. "Surrender, or taste my blade!"

He gave the sack of hay a firm blow with the poker. "That's you taken care of," he announced. "One day I'll be the finest swordsman in all Avantia. Even better than my father, Taladon the Swift!"

Tom felt the ache in his heart that always came when he thought about his father. The uncle and aunt who had brought Tom up since he was a baby never spoke about him or why he had left Tom to their care after Tom's mother had died.

He shoved the poker back into his pack. "One day I'll know the truth," he swore.

As Tom walked back to the village, a sharp smell caught at the back of his throat.

"Smoke!" he thought.

He stopped and looked around. Through the trees to his left, he could hear a faint crackling as a wave of warm air hit him.

Fire!

Tom pushed his way through the trees and burst into a field. The golden wheat had been burned to black stubble and a veil of smoke hung in the air. Tom stared in horror. How had this happened?

He looked up and blinked. For a second he thought he saw a dark shape moving towards the hills in the distance. But then the sky was empty again.

An angry voice called out. "Who's there?"

Through the smoke, Tom saw a figure stamping round the edge of the field.

"Did you come through the woods?" the man demanded. "Did you see who did this?"

Tom shook his head. "I didn't see a soul!"

"There's evil at work here," said the farmer, his eyes flashing. "Go and tell your uncle what's happened. Our village of Errinel is cursed – and maybe all of us with it!"

Tom turned and ran as fast as he could, stumbling over the blackened tree roots.

Tom burst into the village square, gasping for breath. It was full of villagers. What were they all doing here? It wasn't market day. They were shouting and waving their hands at his uncle, who was standing on a bench at the edge of the square.

"Fire in the fields! What next?" one man shouted.

"The troubles get worse each day!" called another villager.

"The Beasts have turned evil!"

Tom knew that Avantia was said to be protected by six Beasts, including a fire dragon, but no one was sure if they really existed.

"Have you seen the river?" a woman

asked. "It's so low we will soon run out of drinking water."

"We're cursed," an old man wailed.

"I don't believe in curses," said Tom's uncle firmly. "But our village needs help. One of us must go to the king and request his aid."

Tom stepped forward. "*I'll* go to the palace."

The villagers laughed. "Send a boy on such a mission? Ha!"

"The king would laugh at us for sending a child."

Tom's uncle spoke quietly. "No, Tom. You're too young. I'm head of the village. I'll go."

Suddenly a small boy, smeared in soot, pushed through the crowd. "Help!" he gasped. "Please help! Our barn is on fire!"

"Men! Bring your pails to the river

now!" Tom's uncle roared to the crowd. "The rest of you bring spades to the barn – if we can't quench the fire we'll bury it. Quickly!"

Tom looked at his uncle as the men rushed to obey. "The village needs you here as its leader, Uncle Henry," he said. "Please let me go instead."

Tom's uncle turned to face him, his face serious. "I suppose I have to let you out into the world sooner or later," he said. He stared into the distance. "Perhaps it's meant to be..." He shook himself and turned back to Tom. "Yes, you must go to the king. And there is no time to waste – you will have to leave first thing tomorrow!"

Fight the Beasts,
Fear the Magic

www.beastquest.co.uk

Have you checked out the Beast Quest website?
It's the place to go for games, downloads, activities,
sneak previews and lots of fun!

You can read all about your favourite beasts,
download free screensavers and desktop wallpapers
for your computer, and even challenge your friends
to a Beast Tournament.

Sign up to the newsletter at www.beastquest.co.uk
to receive exclusive extra content and the
opportunity to enter special members-only
competitions. We'll send you up-to-date info on all
the Beast Quest books, including the next exciting
series which features four brand-new Beasts!

Series 14: THE CURSED DRAGON
COLLECT THEM ALL!

Tom must face four terrifying Beasts as he
searches for the ingredients for a potion to
rescue the Cursed Dragon.

978 1 40832 920 7

978 1 40832 921 4

978 1 40832 922 1

978 1 40832 923 8

SPECIAL BUMPER EDITION: OKAWA THE RIVER BEAST
Coming in May 2014!

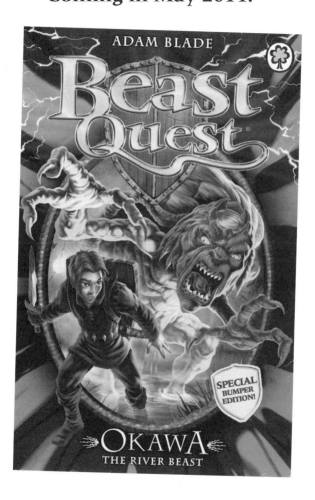

Watch out for another new
Special Bumper
Edition
OUT OCTOBER 2014!

Reading Tips

National Literacy Trust

The **National Literacy Trust** is a charity that transforms lives through literacy. We want to get more families reading. Reading is fun and children who read in their own time do better at school and later in life. By partnering with McDonald's, we hope to encourage more families to read together.

Here are some of our top tips for reading with children.

- A good way to bring a book to life is to put on different voices for different characters in the story.

- Why not stop at certain points in the story to ask your child what *they* think will happen next?

- Setting aside some time to read with your child every day is something both of you can look forward to.

- A shared love of reading can last a lifetime. You can still read aloud to your child, even when they are confident enough to read by themselves.

- If your child is excited by the subject of a story, it will help keep their interest as you read together, so help them choose the books you'll read together.